W9-AOC-109

THE MISSING MOTHER GOOSE

...

STEPHEN KRENSKY

ILLUSTRATED BY
CHRIS DEMAREST

DOUBLEDAY

NEW YORK LONDON TORONTO SYDNEY AUCKLAND

PUBLISHED BY DOUBLEDAY
a division of Bantam Doubleday Dell Publishing Group, Inc.
666 Fifth Avenue, New York, New York 10103

DOUBLEDAY
and the portrayal of an anchor with a dolphin
are trademarks of Doubleday, a division of
Bantam Doubleday Dell Publishing Group, Inc.

DESIGNED BY DIANE STEVENSON/SNAP•HAUS GRAPHICS

LIBRARY OF CONGRESS CATALOGING-IN-PUBLICATION DATA

Krensky, Stephen.
The missing Mother Goose / Stephen Krensky ; illustrated by Chris Demarest. — 1st ed.
p. cm.
Summary: A collection of seven stories based on
favorite Mother Goose rhymes, including expanded versions
of "Humpty Dumpty," "Little Miss Muffet," and "Old King Cole."
1. Tales. [1. Nursery rhymes—Adaptations. 2. Folklore.]
I. Demarest, Chris L., ill. II. Title.
PZ8.1.K866M1 1991
398.2—dc20
[E] 90-14102 CIP AC
ISBN 0-385-26273-6
ISBN 0-385-26274-4 (lib. bdg.)
R.L. 3.1

Printed in Hong Kong

October 1991
First Edition

CONTENTS

...

OLD KING COLE

Old King Cole
Was a merry old soul,
And a merry old soul was he;
He called for his pipe,
And he called for his bowl,
And he called for his fiddlers three.

■ ■ ■

Old King Cole was a merry old soul. And he had every reason to be. He slept late each morning. He wore comfortable clothes that never itched. And he put his elbows on the table whenever he wanted.

The happy king tried to look on the bright side of things and encouraged others to do the same. So while his kingdom had the usual fights and disagreements, the king settled most of them peacefully in very short order.

Amid the general peace and prosperity, the king was a great favorite with everyone—everyone, that is, except his daughter, Princess Emma. She was very prim and proper, with strict notions of how royalty should behave.

Almost every day Princess Emma complained to her father about something. His clothes were too wrinkled. His hair wasn't brushed. His wretched pipe constantly fouled the air in the throne room. She didn't mind that he ate with his fingers—everyone did that—but she turned beet-red whenever he slurped his soup.

The king always stopped to hear his daughter out, and he never took offense at anything she said. But he never followed her advice, either.

On Princess Emma's sixteenth birthday, the king decided to give the princess a very special present.

"I will grant you a wish," he told her. "Any wish within my power. What shall it be? New clothes? A summer house? Jewels, perhaps?"

Princess Emma was delighted, but not because she wanted a different dress or more diamonds. "I know just what I want," she said. "I want you to act like a proper and dignified king."

The king frowned. "Wouldn't you rather have a necklace?"

"No," said the princess. Her mind was made up.

Old King Cole sighed. He did not much care for her wish, but a promise was a promise.

Princess Emma began making changes at once. She ordered the royal tailor to make her father a set of heavy woolen robes with stiff collars. She ordered the royal cook to stop serving dessert first. And she told the king himself he could no longer put his feet up on the furniture.

The king protested. "But it's so often the best place to put them."

The princess remained firm. "No feet," she said.

The king tried bravely to conform. He sat up straight in chairs, ate plenty of vegetables, and only pulled at his collar when the princess wasn't looking.

In his current mood, though, Old King Cole had no patience for settling disputes. Before long his jails and dungeons were full of feuding farmers and battling townsfolk. The mood in his castle was no better. Footmen were fighting with chamberlains, chamberlains with valets, and valets with ladies-in-waiting.

The princess was aware of all this, but she thought it was a price worth paying. She was very pleased that the king had reformed.

She was not so pleased one morning, though, when the king forbade her to go horseback riding.

"I have no escort available," he explained. "And you may not go without one."

"I am in no danger here," said the princess.

Her father folded his arms. "It is not a question of danger, it is a matter of appearances. And appearances are most important, or so you've always said."

The princess had no answer to that.

This was just the beginning. At meals the king hired a royal food taster to sample everything first. By the time the princess got her food, it was always cold. The king also ordered her to wake up every day at dawn and travel around the countryside meeting her subjects.

"We must set an example to the people," he said. "If we work hard, they will, too."

After a whole month of this, Princess Emma couldn't stand it anymore. All of her time was spoken for. She hardly ever saw her friends, and she was constantly yawning. It was no good making her father behave properly if the rest of her life was ruined as a result.

At dinner that night, she told the king that she was giving up her birthday wish.

Old King Cole was cautious.

"No more stiff collars?" he asked.

She nodded.

"No more spinach stews?"

She nodded.

"No more keeping my feet off the furniture?"

The princess paused. "Very well," she sighed.

That night Old King Cole sat on his throne in an old robe with frayed sleeves, finishing his third piece of cake. He was quite content. With a sweep of his hand, he called for his pipe, and he called for his bowl, and he called for his fiddlers three. Princess Emma sat at his side, trying to convince herself she had done the right thing.

As the three fiddlers started to play, the king settled back in his chair. It was good to be merry again. He dangled a slipper on his toe and hummed happily out of tune.

HEY DIDDLE
DIDDLE

Hey diddle diddle,
The cat and the fiddle,
The cow jumped over the moon;
The little dog laughed
To see such sport,
And the dish ran away with the spoon.

■ ■ ■

In a small house at the forest's edge there lived a blacksmith. He had a hot temper to match the fire in his forge, and no one could stand his company for very long. Even his cat and his dog liked each other better than they liked him.

One evening a passing traveler knocked at the blacksmith's door. He was looking for a place to take shelter for the night.

"Do you have any money?" the blacksmith asked.

"None to spare," the traveler replied. "But I can sing you a song for your trouble." He pointed to the back of the room. "Or I could play the fiddle you keep in that cupboard."

The blacksmith gawked at him. "How do you know of the fiddle? I haven't played it since I was a boy."

The traveler simply shrugged. "If music is not to your taste, I could sweeten your well water or—"

But the blacksmith would hear no more. "We'll have no hocus-pocus here," he declared.

The traveler shivered in his cloak.

"If need be," he said, "I will stay in the barn."

"My cow sleeps in the barn. So does my dog. They would not welcome your company. Now, be off with you!"

Having said that, the blacksmith slammed the door in the traveler's face.

The traveler shook his head and retreated to the road. The blacksmith, he thought, needed a lesson in both magic and manners.

A short while later the blacksmith finished his chores and set to making his supper. He chopped up

an onion and some carrots, putting them in a thin soup cooking over the fire.

Suddenly, the wind blew the door open. It ruffled the cat's tail, swept a dish and spoon off the table, and opened the cupboard wide.

The cat jumped up at once and took down the fiddle.

"Here now, Puss," said the blacksmith, "you stop that."

The cat paid him no mind. She tucked the fiddle under her chin and began to play. The blacksmith always threw shoes at her when she tried to sing along with the other cats. Now she would show him a thing or two.

"It's a trick!" the blacksmith declared.

Trick or not, the fallen dish and spoon suddenly rose and began dancing on the floor. The blacksmith never cleaned them properly. They were glad of the chance to shake off the dirt and grime.

The blacksmith might have scooped them both up, but he heard his dog barking and his cow mooing. He rushed out to the barn to see what was the matter.

As the blacksmith opened the barn doors, his cow trotted past him. The light of the full moon fell across her horns, and she began to prance about, first one way and then the other. It wasn't right that the blacksmith only thought of her for milk. She was good for more than that.

With a mighty jump, the cow leaped up into the sky.

The blacksmith stared and stared.

The cat was still playing the fiddle. The dish was still dancing with the spoon. The little dog was running around in a circle, laughing at everyone.

The blacksmith said nothing. He stood there, his neck craned upward, watching his cow jump over the moon. His dish and spoon danced right past him, and then ran away into the forest.

The blacksmith did not give chase. He stumbled back into his house and went to bed without any supper. He didn't see his cow land softly in the nearby field, where she mooed to the dog about the wonders she had seen.

Some time later, the dish and the spoon arrived at the traveler's campsite. He was sitting on a log, stirring a pot of stew.

"Just in time," he said.

He put the stew on the dish, and with the help of the spoon had himself a fine meal.

JACK BE NIMBLE

Jack be nimble,
Jack be quick,
Jack jump over
the candlestick.

■　■　■

J ack was the youngest of three brothers who lived together in a small cottage in the woods. His two older brothers, Simon and Ned, were both fat and lazy and very good at ordering Jack around. Jack himself was lean and hardworking and very good at doing what he was told.

There were hardly enough hours in the day for Jack to do everything his brothers wanted. There were fields to tend, meals to cook, and clothes to wash. Sometimes Jack was so hurried, he weeded the garden with one hand and whitewashed the fence with the other.

One morning at breakfast Ned had news.

"There's going to be a country fair tomorrow."

Simon rubbed his hands. "That means a pie-eating contest. I almost won last year."

Jack said nothing. He too wanted to go to the fair, but he knew he would have to finish his chores first.

The next day Jack got up before there was any day to speak of. He washed the floor, darned the socks, milked the cow, and hitched the horse to the wagon before his brothers finished breakfast. He had not finished repairing the stone wall, though, when they were ready to leave.

"I guess you'll have to walk, then," said Simon. He and Ned laughed as they left in the wagon.

The morning was half gone before Jack started off. He had not gone far when he came upon a tinsmith whose cart was stuck in a ditch. Jack stopped to help get the cart back onto the road. In return the grateful tinsmith gave Jack a ride to the fair.

The fair was full of noise and color. People haggled over silks and fat pigs, their voices reflecting their delight or disappointment. There were entertainers, too, and Jack watched as a fire-eater swallowed four torches and a man juggled five potatoes blindfolded.

One peddler had drawn a crowd by offering a bag of gold to anyone who could leap over a lighted candlestick without extinguishing the flame.

"Anyone can try for the price of a shilling," he was saying. "Come on, who'll be next?"

Many farmers and townsfolk were eager to take a chance. Some of them cleared the candlestick by inches, others by a foot. But all of them blew out the flame.

"There's a trick to it," said a voice behind Jack.

Jack turned. It was the tinsmith, the one he had met on the road.

"Well, not a trick exactly," the tinsmith continued. "You must be nimble and quick enough to twist at the last moment and pull up your legs. Can you do that?"

"I think so," said Jack. It was not so different from setting the table with one hand and sweeping the floor with the other. "But I have no shillings to wager."

"Ah, but I do," said the tinsmith. "You saved me a great deal of trouble this morning. Let me return the favor."

"Anyone else?" the peddler asked, pocketing yet another coin.

Jack stepped forward. "I'll give it a try," he said.

Simon snorted. "Pay him no mind," he said. "He has no money to play with. He—"

Simon choked on his next words as Jack held up a shilling.

"All right, step back," said the peddler. "Give him room."

Jack measured his stride against the distance. Then he carefully picked his starting point. Taking a deep breath, he made his approach.

Up, up, and over he went, twisting around and pulling in his legs.

The flame flapped twice, but stayed lit.

"Hurrah!" said the crowd. "Hurrah!"

"You see," said the peddler, who wasn't as sad as he might have been. One winner was always good for business. "A mere lad has done it. Now who'll be next?"

Jack took the bag of gold and looked around. He wanted to share his good fortune with the tinsmith.

But the tinsmith was gone.

Simon and Ned, however, came quickly to his side.

"Brother, that bag must be heavy," said Simon. "Let me hold it for you."

"Or me," said Ned. "You are not big enough to keep it safe. I will guard it for you."

Jack pulled loose from them both. "Don't worry," he said. "I won't have it long. I'm going to buy a small farm and be my own master."

And that's just what he did. He invited Simon and Ned over for dinner once a week, but otherwise they had to fend for themselves. Neither of them was ever able to jump over a lighted candlestick, but they both became a bit more nimble and quick in the future.

HUMPTY DUMPTY

Humpty Dumpty sat on a wall,
Humpty Dumpty had a great fall.
All the king's horses
And all the king's men
Couldn't put Humpty together again.

■ ■ ■

There was once a traveling performer whose name was Humpty Dumpty. Humpty was small at the top and small at the bottom and rather round across the middle. This was a good shape for being shot out of cannons and going over waterfalls in a barrel.

Humpty Dumpty went far and wide doing his stunts. And wherever he went, people were amazed.

"Ooooooh!" they cried, when he vaulted through a burning hoop.

"Aaaaaah!" they shouted, when he rode a horse while standing on his head.

The more stunts Humpty did, the more famous he became. After every performance, the audience crowded round to shake Humpty's hand.

"You're very brave," they said.

"Thank you," said Humpty. "Thank you very much."

There came a day, though, when the mood of the crowd changed.

The "Oooohs!" became few and far between.

The "Aaaahs!" were gone altogether.

The problem was that Humpty made everything look easy. People were no longer surprised when he balanced spears on his nose or caged himself with a lion. When Humpty locked himself in a dungeon with a keg of gunpowder and no key, only two boys and a dog stayed to see him escape before the explosion.

That was too much for Humpty. Disappointed in his audience, Humpty stopped performing and went home. He was very upset. Humpty had always planned his tricks perfectly, but he had never planned on having people take him for granted.

From his balcony in the town, Humpty watched the crowds passing below. He sat down on the edge, carelessly dangling his legs over the side.

"Things will never be the same," he thought. It made him sad.

A few people saw Humpty sitting there. He looked nervous, they thought. And worried, too. They had never seen Humpty look nervous and worried.

"Maybe he's going to try something spectacular," they thought. "Something that frightens even him."

The news spread quickly.

Blacksmiths dropped their horseshoes and came running. Bakers left bread burning in the oven. Tailors deserted clients standing in their underwear.

Soon, the king's horses and the king's men arrived to see what all the excitement was about.

People tried to guess what Humpty would do.

"Maybe he'll walk down the wall on his hands," said some.

"Or jump onto the back of a galloping horse," said others.

The buzz of voices roused Humpty from his thoughts. He looked down. His audience had returned after all. He had missed the crowds more than he cared to admit. Obviously they had missed him too.

Humpty decided to make a speech.

"My friends . . ." he began, and then paused. For a proper speech, he really should stand up.

As he started to rise, though, his mind was on his next words and not on where he was putting his feet.

The next moment Humpty slipped and fell.

The crowd gasped.

"Did you ever see such a thing?"

"He didn't even try to save himself!"

"What an act!"

Humpty didn't get up from the ground right away. He had had a great fall.

Many people rushed forward to help. But even all the king's horses and all the king's men couldn't put Humpty Dumpty together again—at least not exactly the way he had been before. He could walk and talk as well as ever, but life was not the same. Humpty knew

he could never top this latest stunt, not in the eyes of his public.

So he retired.

The townspeople said they understood, and maybe some of them did.

"We'll tell our children about him," they said. "And our grandchildren too."

Humpty moved to a small cottage in the country where his ribbons and trophies stood proudly on the mantel. He read a lot of books and grew prizewinning vegetables in his garden.

On holidays he still swallowed swords and juggled pies for neighboring children. Humpty Dumpty never did any more tricks from the top of a wall, but the children didn't seem to mind.

LITTLE MISS MUFFET

Little Miss Muffet
Sat on a tuffet,
Eating her curds and whey;
There came a big spider,
Who sat down beside her
And frightened Miss Muffet away.

■ ■ ■

In the garden of the Muffet family lived a spider who had grown big and fat from eating a great many flies. He ate flies for breakfast, flies for lunch, and flies for dinner. He even ate flies when all he wanted was a little snack.

Not surprisingly, the spider finally grew a little tired of flies and longed for something else. But unsure of what this something might be, he decided to spin an enormous web and see what he would catch.

He began this web early one morning, spinning it between the branch and trunk of an apple tree. After he finished, he sat down above it to wait. He was very good at waiting.

Inside the house Little Miss Muffet—Patience, to her friends—was coming down to breakfast. It was a fine day, or so she thought until her mother put a bowl in front of her.

"What's that?" asked Patience. She didn't like the look of it.

"Curds and whey," said her mother. "It's good for you."

Patience made a face. It was a bad sign when her mother said that. Only the day before, she had used the same words while serving up some liver and spinach pie.

"It doesn't smell good," said Patience. Maybe her cat Scamper would like it. Cats liked milk, and curds and whey were like milk, in a second-cousin-once-removed sort of way.

"No excuses, missy. Eat it here or take it out, but I want you to finish that bowl."

Patience sighed. There was no use arguing with her mother when she used that tone. But at least outside she wouldn't have to smell the stuff.

She picked up her bowl and spoon. "I'll be in the yard," she said.

Patience shut the garden gate, frowning at the bright sunshine.

"Maybe," she thought, "I could pretend the curds and whey were a great delicacy." She looked at the bowl. The floating curds looked too mushy to be any kind of special treat.

   "Or," she said quickly, "it could be a magical porridge that will give me wisdom and beauty." She looked again at the bowl. The milky whey did not seem very wise or beautiful.

   Patience was much too busy thinking to pay attention to where she was going. And so she didn't see the spider's web until it was too late.

   "Yuck," she said.

   She sat down on a tuffet and wiped the sticky threads off on the grass. The curds and whey were going to be awful, she just knew it. But what could she do? Her mother was watching her every move through the window.

Suddenly Patience froze.

A spider had dropped down beside her. He had known he had caught something in his web. Now he was coming to investigate.

He looked at this big creature before him. It certainly was ugly, not like a fly at all.

Patience just stared. This was the biggest spider she had ever seen. It was so big even her mother could see it from the window.

Now Patience didn't have strong feelings about spiders, even big ones, one way or the other. But her mother didn't know that. This was the chance Patience had been waiting for.

She screamed loudly, dropping the bowl in the grass. "A spider!" she cried. Then she jumped up and ran away.

The startled spider dropped into the grass. What a terrible noise the creature made! He took a quick look in the discarded bowl, but the cat was coming and so he scuttled off into the grass.

When Patience returned, Scamper was disappearing around the corner of the house, licking whey from her whiskers. The bowl was empty.

Patience was always rather fond of spiders after that. As for the hungry spider, he went back to catching flies. Everything else was more trouble than it was worth.

HICKORY, DICKORY, DOCK

Hickory, dickory, dock,
The mouse ran up the clock.
The clock struck one,
The mouse ran down,
Hickory, dickory, dock.

■ ■ ■

There was once a mouse who came to live in the stone wall behind an old farmhouse. He thought himself a very clever mouse, and as mice go, he was probably right.

Every night, when everyone in the farmhouse was asleep, he scurried inside for his supper. Some nights he got cheese from the pantry. Other nights he got cornmeal from the cupboard. He always checked under the baby's chair because the baby was not a very careful eater.

When the farmer found holes chewed in some storage bags, he knew a mouse was responsible. So he stopped up all the mouse holes he could find and hoped that would be an end to the problem.

But it wasn't. The mouse did not mind that his old holes had been filled in. "I do not need old holes," he thought. "I am too clever for that."

And then he made new holes, in places where nobody found them.

When the farmer saw that the mouse was still getting in, he put out traps—traps with metal springs baited with cheese.

The mouse inspected the traps cautiously. "I would never step in there," he thought, "not even for a nice piece of cheese. I am too clever for that."

When the farmer found his traps empty, he put out wire cages, cages filled with corn and bits of dumpling.

The mouse circled the cages carefully. "I would never step in there," he thought, "not even for corn

and dumplings. I am too clever for that."

For several weeks the mouse did as he pleased because the farmer and his family were fresh out of ideas. They just put up with him as best they could.

One day a large crate was delivered to the farmhouse. Inside was a grandfather clock, left to the farmer by his great-aunt who had recently died. The farmer and his family were delighted to have such a fine old clock, and they put it in the parlor.

That evening, the mouse entered the farmhouse not long after midnight. He heard a strange noise coming from the parlor.

Hickory, dickory, dock . . . Hickory, dickory, dock . . .

What could that noise be? Was it part of another trap? The mouse decided to investigate.

When he entered the parlor, the sound grew louder. He ran to each chair and then under the table. They were all silent.

But what about that wooden box in the corner? It was very tall, so tall that the mouse could barely see to the top.

"Yes," he thought, the *hickory, dickory, dock* was coming from there.

The mouse was puzzled. Except for making the strange noise, the box didn't do anything. It wasn't a trap or a cage. Did the farmer think this would scare him away?

The mouse shook his head. He was not afraid of this box. He ran right up the side. At the top, he scampered about with glee. "They expected this *hickory, dickory, dock* to frighten me," he thought. "But I am not afraid. I am too clever for them." He danced happily from side to side.

Suddenly the clock struck one—and chimed once.

The mouse gasped. The chime was much more than a *hickory, dickory, dock*. It frightened him. Was there some kind of monster in this box? Was it mad at him for dancing on its head? What did the monster like to eat? Mice, perhaps?

The mouse wasn't going to wait around to find out. He was too clever for that. He ran down the clock as fast as he could and left the house.

He didn't come back. The farmer and his family never learned why—and the clock certainly wasn't telling. It just went on ticking *hickory, dickory, dock* for many years to come.

PETER PIPER

Peter Piper picked a peck of pickled pepper;
A peck of pickled pepper Peter Piper picked;
If Peter Piper picked a peck of pickled pepper,
Where's the peck of pickled pepper Peter Piper picked?

■ ■ ■

Peter Piper was a prosperous farmer who planted pumpkins, potatoes, and peppers every year. The pumpkins and potatoes he ate plain, but the peppers he pickled as soon as he picked them. Some people thought he actually grew pickled peppers. This was not true—it just seemed that way.

One sunny day Peter loaded a peck of pickled peppers into his wagon. He planned to take them to market. As he started off, he thought about how pickled peppers made his lips pucker. They certainly were delicious.

"I wonder what I will get for them," he thought. He knew he made the best pickled peppers around. Still, pickled peppers were not to everyone's taste. What if nobody wanted them? What would he do?

At that moment Peter came to a crossroads. He was hailed by a second farmer, who was carrying two buckets of bundled beans on a pole across his shoulders.

"Good day," said the second farmer. He looked in Peter's wagon. "That's a pretty peck of pickled peppers."

"Thank you," said Peter.

The second farmer sighed. "My buckets of bundled beans are heavy," he said.

Peter smiled. He realized he would be far better off with two buckets of bundled beans than a peck of pickled peppers. He needn't worry about whether or not people wanted beans. Everyone ate beans.

"Do you wish to trade?" Peter asked.

The second farmer nodded.

The trade was made, and Peter continued on his way. He whistled happily at his good luck. How easily he would sell the buckets of bundled beans. Of course, beans were not too exciting. Some people probably couldn't be bothered with them. What if only those people came to the market today?

At a fork in the road Peter met a third farmer. The farmer's wagon was filled with a heap of hay.

"Good day," said the third farmer. He sneezed. "Those are beautiful buckets of bundled beans."

"Thank you," said Peter.

The third farmer sneezed again. "This heap of hay is making my nose itch," he explained. "I don't suppose it troubles you."

"No, it doesn't," said Peter. Then he smiled. He would be much better off with a heap of hay than two

buckets of bundled beans. Horses and cows were not so particular about what they ate.

"Do you wish to trade?" Peter asked.

The third farmer sneezed twice and nodded.

The trade was made, and Peter continued on his way. As he reached the outskirts of town, he began to frown. Hay was fine for horses and cows, but horses and cows would not be buying at the market. What if the other farmers were only looking to feed themselves?

A fourth farmer pulled alongside Peter. This farmer's wagon was filled with a mound of melons.

"Good day," said the fourth farmer. "That's a handsome heap of hay you have."

"Thank you," said Peter.

"Lightning struck my haystack and burned it to

the ground. My cows and horses won't eat melons, so I came here to see what I can get for them."

Peter smiled. A mound of melons was a great treat. Everyone loved them. He could trade a mound of melons for anything.

"Do you wish to trade?" Peter asked.

The fourth farmer nodded.

The trade was made, and Peter continued on his way.

Inside the market, he found many booths and stalls to look at. How often did people want to eat melons? Did he have too much of a good thing? What if the melons just sat around and spoiled in the hot sun?

In one of the booths stood a fifth farmer. He was standing in front of a peck of pickled peppers.

"That's a marvelous mound of melons," said the fifth farmer.

"Thank you," said Peter.

The fifth farmer rubbed his chin. "Melons are most refreshing," he said.

Peter smiled. He liked melons as much as anyone, but pickled peppers were something special. "Did you grow these yourself?" he asked. "They look very fine."

"Can't say that I did. Swapped them for a ton of tomatoes."

"Do you wish to trade?" Peter asked.

The farmer nodded.

The trade was made, and Peter looked proudly at the back of his wagon. He could not hope to trade for anything better than a peck of pickled peppers. He

loved pickled peppers, especially the way they made his lips pucker. He turned the wagon around and headed for home.

And so where did Peter Piper's peck of pickled peppers end up? Why, in his own stomach, of course, a perfectly proper place for them to be.

NOTES

The true identity of Mother Goose has never been precisely settled. Whoever she was, though, nursery rhymes have been collected in her name for over three hundred years. Many of these rhymes predate the common use of written records, leaving questions about their origins unresolved. There are just enough facts to prompt educated guesses, and through the years plenty of educated people have made them. Most of these guesses were scuttled by Iona and Peter Opie in *The Oxford Dictionary of Nursery Rhymes*, where much of the information that follows was found.

Wherever possible, the stories in this collection include any historical information related to the rhymes themselves. However, since so little is known for certain, the characters were largely free to do as they pleased.

OLD KING COLE

The merry fellow first appeared in print around 1708, but his true ancestry is not known for sure. There was a British King Cole in the third century whose daughter was supposedly fond of music. Among kings named Cole, he is the most likely inspiration for the rhyme, but no proof exists that he is Old King Cole himself. Another candidate is a wealthy clothier of Reading, England, named Cole-brook. Apparently he was so rich he had 140 house servants. Even if he didn't inspire any rhymes, such a kingly existence was certainly something to be merry about.

HEY DIDDLE DIDDLE

The line "Hey-didle-didle" appeared in a play as the name of a dance in 1569. The rest of the rhyme was published around 1765. There have been various attempts to explain the rhyme in connection with stars, natural phenomena, or royal figures such as Queen Elizabeth I. The Opies, however, pointedly cite a comment made by Sir Henry Reid. " 'I prefer to think,' he says, 'that it [the rhyme] commemorates the athletic lunacy to which the strange conspiracy of the cat and the fiddle incited the cow.' "

JACK BE NIMBLE

Candle jumping was actually a sport for several hundred years in England, but it no longer had a large following when this rhyme was first recorded in 1815. Lacemakers from Buckinghamshire also sometimes jumped over candlesticks for luck during the celebration of St. Catherine's Day, November 25th. If the lighted candle stayed lit after the leap, the jumper would have good luck for the coming year. Whether or not this was true, successful jumpers were at least fortunate enough not to have charred their pants.

HUMPTY DUMPTY

The name Humpty Dumpty first appeared as an ale-and-brandy drink in the late 1600s. A person was not described in the sense of the nursery rhyme until a hundred years later. Written references to Humpty's unfortunate fall date from 1803. Although the original egg-like Humpty Dumpty has never been definitively linked with any actual person, there are equivalent characters in other European tales. Whether this means there were once many Humpty Dumptys or just one who traveled a lot remains a mystery.

LITTLE MISS MUFFET

The entomologist Dr. Thomas Muffet, who died in 1604, leads the contenders for being Little Miss Muffet's father. He wrote *The Silkwormes and Their Flies* in verse and was known as a great admirer of spiders. What his daughter Patience thought of them (or of curds and whey) is not known. However, since the earliest mention of the rhyme came in 1805, this leaves a considerable gap between the man and the meter.

HICKORY, DICKORY, DOCK

The medieval shepherds of Westmorland once used the words "hevera," "devera," and "dick" for eight, nine, and ten. And so the rhyme, which appeared in print in the mid-1700s, possibly grew out of a kind of counting exercise. On the other hand, the words "hickory, dickory, dock" may simply be an attempt to imitate the sound of a ticking grandfather clock. Nobody has ever bothered to try to explain the actions of the mouse, and for this mice everywhere are probably grateful.

PETER PIPER

This rhyme first appeared in *Peter Piper's Practical Principles of Plain and Perfect Pronunciation*. The author was not P. Piper, but J. Harris. The fact that the word "pronunciation" begins with the letter "p" may have led backward to the choice of a name. Although this rhyme was published in 1813, similar verses were tripping up tongues for some time before that.

■ ■ ■